JONATHAN STINSON

The School Rewind

Contents

1

Introduction

Welcome to the introduction! Today, you will go on a wild ride with Zing and Connor while they try to stop the days from repeating themselves.

In Chapter 1, you will read Zing's story of how his days keep repeating but the days keep getting shorter and shorter.

In Chapter 2, you will read Connor's story of how his days keep repeating when Connor or anyone else says "dawn."

Then its up to you to find the connection of both of these stories.

Are you ready for a wild ride? Flip to chapter 1 to start your adventure with Zing!

2

Chapter 1: Zing's Story

It's freshman year, and I'm already doing terrible in school. Math, D. Science, C. Other subjects, F. However, today is the last day of the semester, then it's summer break, but I'll have to spend time at summer school since I'm failing.

I walked into school then I blacked out immediately. The only thing I saw while I blacked out was darkness. I was confused. "HA, HA, HA! Good one Joe, you really beat Zing up this time!" Said James when I was standing up. "Wha...WHAT?" I said. "We beat you up real good this time; you need to work on your grades and a better name!" Said Joe. Then, James, Joe, and John walked away laughing.

Those guys were the "Three J's" Bully Group. It consists of Joe, James, and John. If you get made fun of, they're going to bully you until you drop out of high school. I was one of the kids that got made fun of since I have a weird name and terrible grades. So, I was now on the radar of the Three J's...Bummer.

But I might as well get to class now; the time never stops ticking. I walked down the hallway looking at all the cliques, one by one, they started laughing at me when I was walking through the hallway to my homeroom. I was humiliated and ran to my homeroom, avoiding all eye contact. I ran into the door, bumping my head. I looked at the door and it says Book Report Due Today. I totally forgot about the book report.

Suddenly, the Three J's walked up to me and said "Dude, you need to do our book report for us. We totally forgot!" Said John. I was shocked and worried. I think they are going to make me do their work, in under 5 minutes! "Well, too bad! Looks like you have to go to summer school." I said in a worried voice. "Excuses, Excuses! Even though you have no parents, you're doing it for us!" Said James.

I have no parents since they disappeared 2 months ago. We were at laser tag and then the fire alarm went off. I escaped the arena, my parents didn't. So, I have a cardboard house outside a milkshake stand for the rich and everyday people. Every day people destroy because they don't like the homeless hanging around. I was able to get them back though by pick pocketing them and using the money to pay for school.

"START WORKING PEASANT, NO DAYDREAMING!" Said John. I snapped into reality then my pencil was moving as fast as I could move it. If I didn't listen, I would blackout a second time. Then, the bell rang. The 1st hour was starting so I rushed inside and I was greeted by my reading teacher, Mrs. A. "Hey Zing, I saw what happened outside my classroom. I will be excusing you from the book report and I'll give you full credit on the report." I was surprised, she never did things like that before. "Oh....Ok! Thank you so much!" I said. I went to my desk until Mrs. A gave us instructions. I started thinking of what's going to happen in summer school since I'm failing. But, I opened my computer and opened the student grade book. The student grade book is a tool on our chrome books so we can see our grades. Then, my jaw dropped. All of my grades were A's! I refreshed the grade book and my jaw dropped even further because those were my final grades submitted to my report card!

But, everything started getting blurry. Mrs. A echoed "Zing? Zing. ZING!" Then it darkened. Something was not right.

* * *

I'm sitting in a dark room with a light beaming down on me. I'm tied with ropes to my chair, "ZING!" Then it darkened. Something was not right. I'm sitting in a dark room with a light beaming down on me. I'm tied with ropes to my chair, and I cannot move. Then a mysterious man walks up to me. "Who dares to enter my voids?" He asked. "I want to know immediately!" I was frightened by his response. My pants started to turn yellow, and I stuttered, "I...I....I...I have no...clue!" He had a confused look on his face; then it turned into an evil face. "Oh I see, I'll cast a spell on you." He said. "What? Why? Why are you doing that and why am I here?" He disappeared, then a blank screen appeared, then the video played.

Many ages ago, the king of Forbidden started a war that changed all countries' lives forever. He wanted all the land in the world, but the countries fought for their land to be protected. There was bloodshed, gore, and other nasty surprises around the world. He was horrified and got a lot of hatred from his fans after the war was concluded. The king of Forbidden then asked his secret spies to develop a spell to redo the entire day. However, a group of evil spies stole the spell and put the spell onto me, Mr. Mystery. But it was a corrupted spell, so I'm stuck here until I'm set free. I'm forced to cast a spell onto anyone who appears in my voids.

The video paused. Mr. Mystery came back and said in a sad tone, "This is what I'm going through; I'm stuck here unless I get set free. Whoever appears here, I must cast the spell onto who comes into my voids. If the key is found, the spell will be gone, and I'll be set free so find it please!" I was surprised by his response, but then everything started spinning, then it stopped. It was now dark again.

* * *

It's freshman year, and I'm already doing terrible in school. Math, D. Science, C. Other subjects, F. However, today is the last day of the semester, then it's summer break but, I'll have to spend time at summer school since I'm failing.

I walk into school...Wait a minute. The day repeated again; today is the last day of school again. But I met the 3 J group again. "Well, Well, Well, ready to be blacked out again." Said Joe. They punched me, or did they?

I dodged the punch and punched back at Joe. James and John ran, screaming like little girls after Joe fell onto the ground.

Everyone wanted to be my best friend that day, and that was the only day where I had a smile on my face. But it hit me, the days will infinitely repeat, and this book will have no ending since it will repeat. But Mr. Mystery said that if I find the key, the spell will be gone.

* * *

It's freshman year, and I'm already doing terribly in school. Math...WAIT. It repeated again. As I walked into the school, I saw a key on top of the school; it's probably the spell remover key. Then I remembered there was a roof access door at the back of the school. So I ran as fast as I could to the door.

As I was running, the J group tried to punch me and black me out again, but I dodged it and kept running...

* * *

It's freshman year...OH, COME ON. It repeated on me again. But wait, the days are compressing to one point, so I must remove the spell before it is the END OF TIME. So I ran...

* * *

It's freshman year...forget it, I must get to the roof. But I tripped over a spoon and just realized something I could do. I'll throw the spoon at the key, so I put in my pock-

* * *

It's freshmen year...I threw the spoon. My heart was pounding until I heard the key fall and I grabbed it. Suddenly the world was collapsing, then the ground beneath me cracked in ha-

* * *

It's the end of the day. I got the key and saved the end of time. However, I keep getting weird looks from people. It's probably because no one knows about the end of time and the corrupted spell.

I'm walking home, and then I got a notification on my school laptop. I checked, and it says I got a schedule change for the next school year. I gasped about the schedule change because I have Mr. Mystery for the 9th hour at 1:48 PM.

3

Chapter 2: Connors Story

Waking up on a Sunday is so sad. You always have to worry about school the next day. Even worse, I have a test on Monday! I'm supposed to study the events leading to The American Revolution (1775-1783) but I have no idea what the events are. Even worse, I don't even know what the word "events" means.

"Honey, breakfast is ready!" my Mom said. "Coming..." in a darkened voice. I stood up from my bed, stretched, and began heading to the stairs. My house has 2 floors and a basement, but the walls are very narrow. Sometimes I have to squeeze myself into the kitchen because the walls are that narrow.

As I walk down the stairs, my mom yells even louder "Connor, get down here for breakfast please!" Eventually I made it to the kitchen and I sat down waiting for my food. While I wait, I pull out my phone to check the news and see what is going on.

I came across a headline stating "Rewind your day with one click." I clicked on the link and it directed me to the article. I started reading the article and it was about how those college students may be able to rewind their school day with only one button.

But as soon as I was done reading the news article, my mom handed me my breakfast and said "Here you go honey! These are my pancakes with double the syrup!" I was surprised, my mom gave me double syrup! "Oh my goodness, thank you mom!" I said. "No problem, Connor! Now starting eating, the pancakes wont eat themselves!" My mom responded.

I started eating the pancakes with double the syrup when I started thinking about the article I just read. Does it really rewind your day? I think it is total bogus, but does my mom think it is bogus? "Hey mom, have you heard these college students were able to rewind their school day with only one button?"

I think my mom would have seen this article online since it got the news today, so..."Yes honey, I did. It's very interesting what these college students have discovered." I cannot believe my mom heard about this!

But I got distracted when the lawn company arrived and started to cut our grass.

I looked at the lawn company's truck from the window and saw something strange. It says on the truck Dawn's Lawn Company! We fix your lawn at half the price. I immediately started thinking about what 'dawn' means. Is it someone I know? Is it an animal? Something is off. I think I know the name 'dawn' from somewhere.

"Connor? Connor. CONNOR!" My mom yelled. I started to feel like I was going to pass out on my chair. Then I blacked out.I could only hear my mom screaming my name "Connor" as I started fading to black.

Now I see darkness. No sound, no voice, only black. "Dawn...Dawn..." said a voice. That's weird, I thought I couldn't hear any sound. I began thinking it was a voice inside my head. "Dawn...Dawn..." said the voice. Yep, I think it is the voice inside my head.

Then I started hearing the sounds of beeping. Am I in a hospital?

My eyes started to open when I started hearing the beeping sounds. "Connor is waking up! Call the doctors quickly!" said my mom. "Mom, why am I in the hospital?" Before my mom answered the question, the doctor rushed in and started to hook up machinery to my body.

"Mom, what are they doing?" I said.

"They are checking your vitals since you passed out and haven't responded for 8 hours." My mom said,

"I WAS OUT FOR 8 HOURS?" I responded.

I was very sad to hear I was out for 4 hours but I don't understand how I passed out and never responded for 4 hours. Did it have something to do with "dawn" or did something happen to me that my mom is not telling me about?

"Connor, you're all set. You may go home now." said the doctor.

"Wait what?" I responded.

"There's nothing wrong with you, I believe you fainted because you were tired. Now go home!" said the doctor.

I stood up from the bed and walked out of the hospital and into my mom's car. Luckily my house is only 2 miles away and so is my school. "Hey son, when you get home you need to get to bed immediately, you have school tomorrow." Ah man, I forgot I have school tomorrow and that stupid test I never studied for is also tomorrow.

After 5 minutes of driving, I'm finally back at my house. I jumped out of the car and ran upstairs to my bed and started sleeping. Tomorrow is a really big day.

* * *

Today is a big day since I have to take my history test today. I woke up from my bed and took my backpack from my bedroom floor and headed down the stairs to the front door.

"Honey, breakfast is ready!" said mom.

"Mom, I need to get to school as soon as possible! I can't have breakfast." I said.

"No honey, eat your breakfast now or you're not getting McDucks at dawn!" said mom.

* * *

Today is a big day since I have to take my history test today. I woke up from my bed and... Wait. Why am I in my room again? Didn't I go downstairs to the front door seconds ago? I went back down the stairs to the front door and my mom said...

"Honey, breakfast is ready. Please eat breakfast or you will not get food at McDucks at dawn."

* * *

Today is a big day since I...WHY AM I IN MY BEDROOM AGAIN? Wait a minute, when someone says dawn does the day reset again?

* * *

Today is a... Ok, it looks like when I or someone says the D word, the day restarts.

* * *

Today is a... OK, SAYING THE 4TH LETTER OF THE ALPHABET RESTARTS THE DAY TOO? Anyways, when I or someone says the 4th letter, the 1st letter, the 23rd letter, and the 14th letter together in a row, the day restarts.

I stood from my bed, grabbed my backpack and rushed out my door before my mom said the word that restarts the day. I ran the 2 miles to my school, covering my ears so I don't hear the 'word.'

As I was about to enter my school, Billy Junior High School, I ran into Joe by accident.

"Hey Connor! Where's my lunch money?" Said Joe.

"It's up your shirt and leave me alone!"

I ran past Joe and up the stairs to the main entrance until Joe stopped me again.

"You will pay! Meet me after school at the baseball field at dawn."

* * *

Today is a... Seriously, Joe reset my entire day. By the way, Joe is my bully. I met him a couple weeks ago and he started bullying me without notice. I remember one day he pushed me down the stairs and ran away. Plus, he never got in trouble.

I stood from my bed, grabbed my backpack and rushed out my door before my mom said the word that restarts the day. I ran the 2 miles to my school, covering my ears so I don't hear the 'word.'

When I made it to school, I jumped into a nearby bush to hide from Joe. Five minutes went by and I came out of my bush and ran to my classroom. I walked into my classroom and everyone started taking the test.

"Ah Connor, looks like you are late today. Take a seat so I can give you the history test." Said Mr. Mystery.

"Ok" I said.

I took a seat at my desk and looked at Mr. Mystery, getting my test ready. I need to pass this test to pass the class. If I don't pass, I might have to be held back!

Then Mr. Mystery came up to me and handed me my test without any comment.

I had no idea what these questions were, so I am going to guess, on every single question. There were over 100 questions and each question had 4 choices, so the odds are not with me. But I have no choice. I have to guess every single question.

After 30 minutes, I handed in my completed test and waited until everyone else finished their test.

15 minutes go by and Mr. Mystery is telling us our scores. I started dripping sweat like crazy as he came up to me with a post-it note.

"Here is your score Connor!" Said Mr. Mystery.

I read the note and it says:

95% - A

You passed the test, so you may wake up now.

I was confused when it said "You may wake up now." 1 minute later, I started to feel tired. 2 minutes went by, and I blacked out.

* * *

Oh my, it's Sunday already. Sunday is... Wait a minute, it's not Monday? Why did I go back a day? That makes no sense.

Suddenly, my mom came rushing into my room.

"Honey, did you have a bad dream?" said mom.

"Maybe, what time is it right now?" I said.

"Connor, it's almost 5:00 PM."

I was shocked. I slept in for almost 16 hours.

"Also Connor, one of your friends is at the front door."

I was shocked again. I slept in for almost 16 hours and one of my friends is at my front door. Without hesitation, I ran downstairs to the front door. When I was running down the stairs, I almost tripped. But I caught myself and kept running down the stairs.

I opened the door and I couldn't believe who it was.

"Hi Zing! Long time no see!" I said.

About the Author

Hello, my name is Jonathan Stinson and I am an author and publisher. I like to write, create, and publish literary works. As of right now, I am currently in high school and I plan to create more books and literary works.

You can connect with me on:

🌐 https://jrwsportfolio.com